Amy confides in the Roses.

The English Roses

Big-Sister Blues

CALLAWAY ARTS & ENTERTAINMENT

19 FULTON STREET, FIFTH FLOOR, NEW YORK, NEW YORK 10038

PUFFIN BOOKS

Published by the Penguin Group
Penguin Young Readers Group, 345 Hudson Street, New York, New York 10014, U.S.A.
Penguin Group (Canada), 90 Eglinton Avenue East, Suite 700, Toronto, Ontario,
Canada M4P2Y3 (a division of Pearson Penguin Canada Inc.)

Penguin Books Ltd., Registered Offices: 80 Strand, London WC2R 0RL, England

First published in the United States of America by Callaway Arts & Entertainment and Puffin Books, 2008

1   3   5   7   9   10   8   6   4   2

First Edition

Copyright ©Madonna, 2008
All rights reserved.

Produced by Callaway Arts & Entertainment
Nicholas Callaway, President and Publisher
Cathy Ferrara, Managing Editor and Production Director
Toshiya Masuda, Art Director • Nelson Gómez, Director of Digital Technology
Joya Rajadhyaksha, Editor • Amy Cloud, Editor
Ivan Wong, Jr. and José Rodríguez, Production
Kathryn Bradwell, Executive Assistant to the Publisher
Jennifer Caffrey • Publishing Assistant

Special thanks to Doug Whiteman and Mariann Donato.

Library of Congress Cataloging-in-Publication Data is available.

Puffin Books ISBN 978-0-14-241093-6

Printed in the United States of America

www.madonna.com   www.callaway.com   www.penguin.com/youngreaders

All of Madonna's proceeds from this book will be donated to
Raising Malawi (www.raisingmalawi.org), an orphan-care initiative.

Contents

CHAPTER I

Lazy Saturday Afternoons

If you haven't heard of the English Roses by now, something must be terribly, horribly wrong with you. Perhaps you've spent the past few years confined to your room, covered in awful, itchy red spots? Or maybe you've been bedridden with some sort of tragic fever? These are the only possible explanations, for, as everyone who's anyone knows, the English Roses are the cream of the crop that rises to the top of major, awesome, fun girls (that's a cool way of saying they are the freshest girls on the planet). Their names are, in alphabetical order: Amy, Binah, Charlotte, Grace, and Nicole; and they are BFF (which, as even your baby sister knows, means best friends forever! Get with the program!).

spring time in London!

Our story begins on a rather cool and drizzly Saturday afternoon that is typical of springtime in London. The crocuses were beginning to peep their heads out of the ground after a long, cold winter, and the musky scent of the rain-soaked earth made everything seem fresh and new.

This particular afternoon found the English Roses draped, perched, and sprawled out upon every available surface in Grace's bedroom, munching on a Harrison family favorite: corn bread. (You see, Grace is from the United States—Atlanta, Georgia, in fact—and her mother's southern specialties aren't to be missed!)

The only problem with lazy Saturday afternoons is that there never seems to be anything to do, and believe me, the English Roses had already been

Cornbread isn't corny... cornbread is fab.

through a quite-thorough list of options. Among the five of them, everyone had seen every remotely interesting movie playing at the cinema. No one had any allowance money to go shopping (well, except for Charlotte, who always had money, and she didn't want to make the rest of the girls feel left out). It was too wet to do anything fun outdoors. (Grace was already grumpy because her weekly football—that's soccer to you Americans—game was canceled.) There was nothing vaguely entertaining on the telly (that's television for you Americans)—not even a juicy gossip talk show. And they were simply too lazy to go out in the drizzle for any fun treats, especially since Grace's mom had been cooking all day.

So the girls lazed around, gossiping, chatting, and having fun doing nothing in particular. Perched on a beanbag chair, Nicole was flipping through that day's *Times*, announcing headlines to the rest of the girls.

"Oh gosh! They discovered another planet," she reported.

Grace grunted and popped a cheese ball in her mouth.

"Harrods is having a spring sale."

Charlotte nodded, filing her nails.

"Hey!" Nicole said, her blonde ponytail bobbing as she raised her head abruptly, revealing a big grin. "The Royal London Circus is coming next week!"

Amy, who was sprawled out on the floor poring over the latest *Vogue*, couldn't help but roll her eyes. She didn't mean to be rude, but sometimes her friends acted more like third graders than sixth graders! "Come on, Nicole," she said. "Aren't we a little old for that?"

"Well, I know it may sound dumb," Nicole said, somewhat defensively, "but I still get a thrill from seeing all the lion tamers and fire breathers and sword swallowers. After all," she added brusquely, "it is the best show on Earth."

Binah, the group's peacemaker, spoke up quickly. "That's true. I do still love to see the acrobats perform."

"Well, believe me, I know all about it," Charlotte mused. "It's basically the only thing I've been hearing about for weeks and weeks. Patrick the Pest is obsessed!"

Patrick was Charlotte's six-year-old brother. He was always doing those annoying things that, for some reason, little brothers love to do—spitting in her soup; calling her Charlotte Fart-lett; and the worst, making vile, embarrassing noises when she was trying to have important phone conversations. The rest of the English Roses gave her sympathetic looks whenever he was mentioned.

"Hey, next week just happens to be our spring break," Nicole said, taking the opportunity to flip open her ever-present planner. Nicole was by far the most neat and organized member of the English Roses. She was the type of girl who always had her homework assignments perfectly typed weeks ahead of time, who relished the smell of office supply stores, and who couldn't stand to be late to class.

At the words "spring break," each girl couldn't help but take a moment to stare dreamily. Besides maybe "summer vacation" or "snow day," "spring break" were the two best words in the English language, because they meant a whole week off from school! Not that the English Roses loathed school, it's just that everyone needs some time off now and then.

"Well, if it's during spring break, I can't go anyway," Amy said, smoothing her T-shirt (her favorite, her mum's vintage Rolling Stones shirt) and sighing dreamily. "I'll be in Milan, Italy, for Fall Fashion Week."

It was the rest of the Roses' turn to roll their eyes. Fall Fashion Week was all Amy had been talking about for the past four months, ever since her mum surprised her for Christmas with tickets to the big event. Fall Fashion Week was the most exciting thing, like, *ever* for the fashion world. And as an aspiring fashion designer herself, Amy was very much hoping to be a part of that world.

"I still don't get it," Grace said. "You're going to Fall Fashion Week?" She gestured out the window. "It's spring!"

"Oh, that," Amy said, waving her hand dismissively. "They show the fall fashions in spring," she explained, "so that store buyers, like my mum, and other fashionistas have time to purchase stuff before fall actually starts."

"Ah-ha," chorused the other Roses, nodding in agreement. That did make sense.

"So, how's your mum doing with the baby and everything?" asked Grace. "It's coming pretty soon, right?"

Amy, whose mum was almost nine months pregnant, was happy about the baby, but she was honestly getting a wee bit tired of everyone constantly asking her about it. She wouldn't dare tell anyone that, though.

"Oooh, do you know if it's a boy or a girl yet?" Binah gushed. Since Binah was an only child, she found the possibility of a new sibling exciting.

"Wouldn't it be cool if it was a girl, Amy?" Nicole sighed. "You could probably design the cutest little outfits for her."

Amy shrugged and concentrated on picking a piece of lint from her jeans. "We don't know yet," she said flatly. "Mum and Richard want it to be a surprise." Richard was Amy's stepfather. Amy's parents had divorced when she was only six years old; and though she lived with her mum, Amy was still very close to her dad, whom she saw every other weekend.

Just then Grace's older brother, Matthew, popped his head into the room. "THINK FAST, Grace," he shouted, chucking a football in her direction.

With expert precision, Grace swiftly gave the ball a thump with her head, sending it flying back into her brother's arms. "Nice try, playa hater," she scoffed. "But no one can get one by me."

At the sight of Grace's brother, Amy had

immediately sat up straight and smoothed her T-shirt. She began running her hand through her curls, throwing him a big smile. The other girls exchanged humorous looks. Amy had always had a crush on Matthew, and the English Roses loved to tease her about it.

"Mom wanted me to tell you that dinner's in an hour . . . if your friends want to stay, they can." He gave the rest of the Roses a quick wave, then disappeared.

Grace sighed. Brothers!

"Your brother is sooo cute, Grace," Amy drawled, twirling a lock of hair happily. Cute boys always made rainy days seem better.

Charlotte giggled. "You're completely boy crazy, Amy!" she said.

"I am not!" Amy countered. "I just happen to appreciate the cute ones!"

Just then, a cacophony of break beats rang out from Amy's purse.

The rest of the girls looked baffled. "Where is that noise coming from?" Grace asked.

"Sorry, it's my new mobile!" Amy answered breathlessly, pawing through her massive leather hobo bag and finally dumping its contents—mostly hair clips, lip glosses, compacts, and old fashion magazines—all over Grace's carpet. Nicole looked absolutely horrified at Amy's lack of organization.

Finally, Amy found her phone and clicked it open. "Hello? Oh, hi Richard." She made a face. "Yeah, I'm at Grace's. Okay. Yep. See you."

"What did Richard want?" Binah wondered.

Amy's mum had married Richard two years ago, and though she had slowly warmed up to the idea of another man in her mum's life, Amy still wasn't exactly thrilled with him. Richard was nothing like her real daddy, who was energetic and fun and completely fabulous. Richard wore dull, pin-striped suits every day, watched only news shows on the telly, and always had his nose buried in *The Wall*

Street Journal. He was sort of like an adult robot. Amy couldn't see what her mum thought was so great about him, but she had finally learned to accept him. They weren't exactly close, however, which was what made the phone call so strange.

Amy hopped up from her place on the floor, dusted off her jeans, threw her things into her bag, and slung it over her shoulder. "I dunno," she said. "He says he needs me at home. Not sure what that means . . ." She made another face—a supremely vile one, I might add. Amy was quite talented at face making. "I'll see you girls on the flip side," she said as she flicked her hair behind her shoulder and strutted out the door. (I should note here that Amy never walked, tiptoed, or skipped. She had a strut. She was famous for it all over school.)

CHAPTER 2

Fashion Disaster

Amy arrived home to find Richard and her ten-year-old sister, Chloe, sitting around the dinner table eating Chinese food from white cartons. Takeout wasn't that unusual at their house since both Richard and Amy's mum worked and were usually too busy to cook; but

btw... this is what Chloe looks like

what was odd was seeing just the two of them eating, since a fuss was always made about the family having dinner together.

Amy heaved her bag onto the table and removed her huge sunglasses. "Where's mum?" she asked.

Richard motioned for her to sit down. "Care for some moo shu chicken?" he asked.

Amy gingerly picked up the container of chicken. She glanced over at Chloe, who, for once, wasn't saying anything. This was strange indeed, as Chloe was usually a nonstop gabber—even more so than Amy! (She also was constantly copying Amy's style. It drove Amy completely bonkers. A girl's style is sacred!)

Something weird was happening. Amy could sense it.

She eyed Richard suspiciously. "What's going on? Where's mum?"

Richard finished chewing, took a sip of soda, and wiped his mouth. "Your mum is upstairs resting. She just got back from the doctor's office, and she's not feeling too well."

Amy got a funny feeling in the pit of her stomach—kind of like when she had the flu, but worse. "Not feeling well?" she repeated, worried. "Is she okay?"

"She's going to be fine," Richard said firmly. "There are some complications with the pregnancy—"

Richard didn't even finish what he was saying. Amy was off and running up the stairs before he had the chance.

Her mum's bedroom door was shut, so she knocked softly. "Mummy?"

"Amy-Paimey, is that you?" came her mother's muffled voice. Amy threw open the door to find her mum, who was usually so fashionable and funky and put-together, looking pale under a mountain of blankets. Her red hair—the exact same shade as Amy's, though not quite as curly—lay across the white pillow in ribbons.

Amy ran to her mother and plopped down on the bed. "What's wrong?" she asked. "Are you okay? Richard won't tell me anything."

"He just doesn't want to upset you," Amy's mother replied. "Everything's fine. I went to the doctor today, and there are some complications with the baby."

Ryan Hudson is T.D.F.—to die for!

Amy felt tears forming in her eyes and heat rising to her face. That sick feeling in her stomach grew worse. "What do you mean, 'complications'?" she asked.

"It's just hypertension," her mum soothed. "I'm too stressed from work, and the baby is feeling it, that's all. So I'm going to have to stay in bed for a while."

"But . . . but . . . just how long is 'a while'" asked Amy, aghast.

"Well, that's something we have to discuss, sweetie," Amy's mum replied, looking down. "I won't be able to take you to Milan next week."

Amy could feel her heart sinking in her chest. All of the air seemed to go out of her lungs at once. No Fashion Week? "But . . . but, I've been looking forward to it for so-o-o lo-ong." And with the last syllable, her voice cracked. She couldn't help it. Amy Brook was not one to cry (that was for babies, and besides, crying made you look like a red-faced freak!), but this horrible news was enough to cause her to break out in heaving sobs.

"Oh, Aimers," her mum said. "I'm so, so sorry. I know how much you were looking forward to it. I promise we'll go next season, once the baby's born."

Amy raised her head and blew her nose loudly into her mother's shirt. She took a deep breath and tried her best to compose herself. "That's okay, mum," she said shakily. "Just as long as you feel better. That's all that matters to me." As soon as she said the words, she realized that they were true.

Though she still felt a pang of disappointment deep in her heart, she just wanted her mum to be okay.

"That's my girl!" her mother said, smiling. "My number one daughter."

Amy smiled. Her mother always told her she was number one. She knew that she meant number one as in oldest, but privately, Amy always fancied that it meant she was number one in her heart, too.

"Oh, and I brought you a surprise from work today," she said, winking. "It's on your bed."

Amy ran into her room to find a Marks & Spencer shopping bag on the bed. (Her mum was a buyer for the largest clothing store in England, which meant that she was responsible for stocking fabulous

clothes and accessories. Can you imagine a more divine job?) Inside was a bottle of the brand-new Stella McCartney perfume, the one that wouldn't hit the stores until summer.

"Mummy, you rock my world!" she screamed, running to her mother and hugging her fiercely. "How did you get it?"

"The fragrance buyer owed me one," her mum said, smiling. "I knew you would love it." Stella McCartney was Amy's idol and ultimate fashion inspiration.

Amy's smile was so wide it seemed to fall off her face. The new Stella McCartney perfume was almost good enough to knock out the bad news about not going to Fashion Week.

Almost.

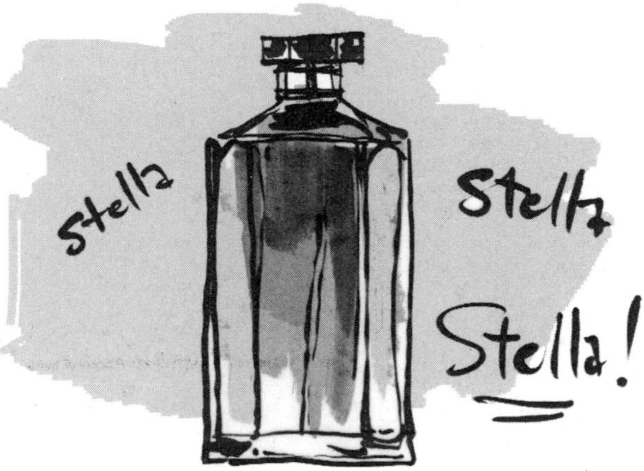
stella
Stella
Stella!

CHAPTER 3

Seize the Day

"Mmmm . . . you smell lovely, Miss Amy," Charlotte said, putting her arm protectively around her friend.

The English Roses were walking to school the Monday after their lazy Saturday. It was still drizzly, still gray, but with the promise of spring break just a few days away, the girls had a lit-tle bounce in their steps.

All the girls except for Amy, that is. She just couldn't seem to get over the fact that she wasn't going to Milan. Do you know the feeling when you're really, really looking forward to something and suddenly it's not going to happen, but for some silly reason you keep forgetting? You wake up in the morning thinking everything's fine, before the horrible reality sets in. Yeah, this was kind of like that. Though she was happy her mum was going to be okay, Amy couldn't help but feel angry. Angry that this baby, whom she didn't even know yet, was affecting her life in such a negative way. Angry that this baby was possibly, maybe, going to hurt her mother. Angry that this baby was coming at all!

She had told the English Roses the whole heart-breaking story during one of their (quite frequent) five-way phone conversations the previous day. Of course, the Roses all gave her not only their caring ears and words of sympathy, but assured her that, no matter what, they would see to it that Amy's

BROWNIES aRe just as fab as Cornbread (maybe even MORE)...

spring break was the most rockin' one yet. Because that's just what best friends do.

The girls tried their best to cheer Amy on the way to school. Charlotte wouldn't stop gushing about how great she smelled, Grace told funny stories about Matthew, Nicole promised that she'd help Amy with her science project, and Binah had shown up with a batch of brownies baked especially for Amy.

"You girls are so sweet!" Amy said. "I don't know what I did to deserve such awesome friends."

Soon the Roses arrived at the school's entrance. They were waiting for the bell to ring when Miss Fluffernutter, their beloved fifth-grade teacher,

bounced by. As usual, she was a bundle of energy, with her hair wrangled into two puffy braids and a mass of papers clutched in her arms. She was holding a bright-colored coffee mug that said SEIZE THE DAY in big black letters.

"Oh hello, my favorite sixth-grade girls!" Miss Fluffernutter buzzed, giving each of the English Roses a big hug.

"Hi, Miss Fluffernutter," the girls chorused.

"How are you today?" added Binah.

"I'm well as well can be!" Miss Fluffernutter squealed in delight. "A dear friend of mine surprised me with tickets for the Royal London Circus next week. I can't wait to go!"

Amy stared in disbelief. "You mean, you still go to the circus, Miss Fluffernutter?"

Miss Fluffernutter looked confused. "Why, yes," she said. "Why ever would I NOT?"

"Well, it's just that, uhh." Amy felt flustered. "You're, you know, a teacher."

"If you're trying to say that I'm too old, I won't hear of it." Miss Fluffernutter smiled.

"Oh no, no, I would never say that, Miss F," Amy said, trying to backtrack.

Miss Fluffernutter opened her mouth and let out a big, booming laugh that seemed to come right from the depths of her heart. "No, you're perfectly right to say that," she said once she had calmed down. "But remember this, girls: you're never too old to have fun." And she trotted away down the hall, hair a-flying, papers flapping, and her loud laugh echoing after her.

Amy couldn't help but smile. *If Miss Fluffernutter liked the circus,* she thought, *it must be a good time!*

Class was about to begin, so the girls filed into their room and took their seats. Amy opened her sketchbook and started doodling designs that she imagined would be perfect for Fall Fashion Week. Just as she began to get into something pretty interesting the bell rang, and Mrs. Moss, their sixth-grade teacher, abruptly called the class to order by rapping on her desk with a ruler.

"All right, students, time to begin," she barked. "I know that spring break is only a few days away, but we really need to get through this material quickly. Please take out your homework

assignments from the weekend."

Amy heaved a giant sigh as she put away her sketchbook. The truth was, she didn't much care for homework, or for Mrs. Moss. The thing that irked her most about Mrs. Moss was that she had a way of barking commands that made Amy feel like a cow being dragged around by an old, dirty rope. And, let's face it, who wants to feel like that?

Just then, the classroom door slammed. All eyes turned to look as Ryan Hudson, the cutest boy in the sixth grade, nonchalantly shuffled to his seat.

"How kind of you to join us, Mr. Hudson," Mrs. Moss said sharply. "Do you realize that this marks your fifth tardy so far in the semester?"

Ryan slid into his seat behind Amy, and Amy couldn't help but whirl around to stare. He gave her a wink and his signature smile, and her body seemed to melt into a puddle right in her seat.

Ryan Hudson was the kind of boy who could make a girl's heart rate accelerate simply by accidentally brushing against her in the hallway. He had sandy brown hair and beautiful blue eyes framed by long, curly eyelashes; and his nose was dotted with a handful of freckles. When he smiled, which he did a lot, he flashed a row of perfectly white, charmingly crooked teeth.

Girls of all ages flocked to Ryan, offering to complete his homework assignments, bake him treats, and write his term papers. It was all worth it, of course, just to see him wink and smile or to hear his low voice whisper "thanks" in your ear. Amy, however, refused to participate in such silly shenanigans. She always played it cool with Ryan, even though inside she usually felt less than sure of herself around him.

"Sorry, Mrs. Moss," Ryan apologized. "My alarm didn't go off this morning."

The classroom seemed to heave a collective sigh as various girls around the room swooned. Mrs. Moss, however, wasn't swayed by Ryan's charms. "One more tardy, sir," she said, "and you'll find yourself spending all your free time with me." She smiled sweetly. "In detention."

Everyone turned around to stare at Ryan, who shrugged casually, then opened his book. Nothing seemed to faze him.

Mrs. Moss started lecturing about cell structure; but, try as she did, Amy couldn't force herself to concentrate on the lesson. Thankfully, a few minutes later, she felt a tap on her shoulder. She whirled around, and Ryan handed her a folded-up piece of paper. "From Charlotte," he mouthed.

Amy momentarily lost it; but she quickly regained composure, turned back around, and opened the note. Here is what it said:

Clothes swap meet. My house. 4 p.m. today. Bring clothes and accessories you don't want anymore. I'll have food and music. And lots of clothes. Emma gave me some of her old things. Pass it on to all of the other E.R.

fig 12: CHARLOTTE'S Note

(ARIAL VIEW)

Amy grinned and looked at Charlotte, who grinned back. The English Roses had started having clothing swaps last year after Emma, Charlotte's infinitely cool older sister, had suggested it. What happened was this: all the Roses gathered—usually at Charlotte's, since she had the biggest bedroom—and brought any clothes that they were sick of or didn't want anymore. They would then throw everything in a big pile and proceed to try on things, modeling garments in a sort of fashion show. The best part was getting to go home with new-to-you clothes that didn't cost a thing. Binah, whose family didn't have much, couldn't contribute clothes, but she made up for it by bringing treats. And this time it would be especially fun, since Emma was throwing in some of her stuff. If Emma had worn it, it had to be cool!

Amy loved clothes swap meets. *Maybe today wouldn't be so bad after all!* she thought.

CHAPTER 4

Clothes Swap

Four o'clock found Nicole, Amy, Charlotte, Grace, and Binah in Charlotte's bedroom, trying on clothes, listening to music, and munching on goodies prepared by Nigella, Charlotte's family chef, and Binah. (You see, Charlotte's family was what you'd call "Wealthy"

with a capital "W"—they had a chef, a butler, and even a driver.)

"That sweater dress is adorable on you, Amy," Charlotte raved with a sigh. "I wish it fit me like that."

"Well, you look devastating in that silver top that just doesn't seem to go with my hair," Amy replied with a wink. "I'll bet William Worthington will appreciate how it makes your eyes sparkle."

Charlotte blushed furiously but couldn't hide her smile. Though she would never admit it, she had had a crush on William Worthington ever since the school play earlier in the year in which he played Romeo to her Juliet.

Amy noticed that Nicole, Grace, and Binah were whispering about something in the corner.

"Girls, no fair," she said crossly. "Secrets do not make friends!"

The girls turned to her, their faces shining. "We were just discussing an idea that Nicole had," Grace said.

"Yeah," Binah added. "We want to do something special for you over spring break. To make you feel better about missing . . ." She couldn't bring herself to say the words. "You know . . ."

"So," said Nicole excitedly, "after school I called my mum, and she got tickets for us—all of us"— she motioned to the rest of the Roses—"to go to the Royal London Circus on Saturday."

Amy couldn't help but smile. Who wouldn't, with such thoughtful, caring friends?

"Aww, you girls are the best," she said, throwing

her arms around each and every one of them.

"I know you think the circus is for babies," Charlotte jumped in, "but just think of the lights, the glitter, and especially the costumes!"

"That's true," Amy said, thinking it over. "The costumes are pretty amazing."

"Plus, Miss Fluffernutter said she's going, too," Grace said.

"But not on the same day," Nicole interrupted.

"That's right," Grace said. "But still, if Miss Fluffernutter wants to go, you know it has to be a good time!"

Amy giggled, and for the first time since Saturday, she was able to push all the unnerving thoughts about her mum and the baby out of her head. Instead, she realized how lucky she was to have the best friends in the whole wide world. Okay, maybe even in the whole universe!

CHAPTER 5

At the Big Top

The week before a vacation always seems to d-r-a-g by, and this one was no exception. Mrs. Moss seemed especially determined to keep her class working hard, even though all anyone could think about was spring break. But finally, after what seemed like a zillion years, spring break did arrive; and before Amy knew it, it was Saturday, the day of the Royal London Circus. The English Roses were meeting at Charlotte's, where Royston, her dependable family driver, was waiting to escort them to the big event.

Right before she was about to strut out the door, Amy popped her head into her mum's room. "Hey, mum," she said. "Do you think I should wear these shoes to the circus today? Or do you like the purple ones better?"

Amy's mum, who looked exhausted again, was sitting up in bed reading a baby-name book. She glanced at Amy. "Mmm-mm. Honey, I'm sure whatever shoes you're wearing are fine." She went back to her book.

Charlotte explodes!

Amy was too hurt to respond. She hurriedly shut the door, then dashed down the stairs and hurled herself out the front door. Her mum had never, ever ignored her like that—especially when it came to something as important as fashion advice. It's a sign, she worried, a sign of what's to come! She tried to brush the fears from her mind, but like a pesky mosquito, they kept coming back.

Things didn't get any better once she arrived at Charlotte's house. Winston, the family butler, greeted Amy at the door and ushered her into the Ginsbergs' larger-than-life foyer, where the rest of the Roses had already gathered. Charlotte was perched on a velvet chaise longue, looking like someone had just told her that the Queen had passed a ruling banning cupcakes forever. Yes, she was that glum!

"Oh, Amy," she pouted, "you'll never guess what's happened!"

"Mmm . . . what?" Amy asked. She was still upset about her mum's behavior at home.

"We have to take Patrick with us!" she wailed. "His nanny was supposed to take him, but her grandmother died, and she has to go to the funeral!"

Binah tried to look on the bright side. "How bad can he be, Charlie?"

Charlotte shot her a Look. "Oh, you have no idea."

Grace stood up. "Well, we're the English Roses," she declared fiercely. "We've been through everything! We can most definitely handle a six-year-old brother!"

(You have no idea...)

Let's go!

Just then, Patrick barreled into the room, screaming at the top of his lungs, "COME ON, YOU GIRLY STUPIDS! LET'S GO!"

The English Roses gave one another wary looks. Amy wasn't so sure Grace was right about this one!

CHAPTER 6

Patrick the Pest

A half hour later, Royston dropped off the girls at the Circus. They filed into the arena, one after the other, with Charlotte holding onto Patrick's grubby little hand. Suddenly, he stopped dead in his tracks.

"Charlie, look! PEANUTS!" he shrieked as he pointed to a nearby vendor selling the fragrant, roasted treats. Their rich scent wafted through the air. Amy had to admit, they smelled unbelievable!

"I know, Pat." Charlie sighed, tugging on Patrick's arm. "But let's find our seats before we get snacks, okay?"

Patrick refused to budge. He angrily stomped his feet, emitting a shrill scream that caused a few bystanders to stop and stare. "But Nanny Marie PROMISED she'd get me some!"

Charlotte flushed beet red. Miss Manners (as the English Roses called their posh and proper friend) wasn't liking this one bit, but she tried to retain some sense of composure. "All right. All right. Then we'll get you some peanuts," she hissed through clenched teeth. She turned to Amy. "Would you be a dear, please, and get this little brat some peanuts so he'll shut up?"

Amy shrugged. Getting away from Patrick would give her ears a rest, at least. She took the wadded-up bills that Charlotte had thrust into her hand and sauntered up to the peanut vendor. Just as she got in line behind a young couple with a baby, she felt a tap on her shoulder. She whirled around to find herself staring right into the deep blue eyes of . . . Ryan Hudson!

"Hey, Ames." He smiled, flashing his signature smile. "I knew that hair couldn't belong to anyone else! What are you doing here?"

For once Amy was speechless. Inside her stomach, a little man performed backflips. The last person she expected to run into at the circus was the dreamiest boy in school.

"Oh, well, actually, I'm just helping Charlotte take care of her little brother," she explained. She displayed a playful grin that she prayed would make her look calm and collected. Anything to hide the fact that she was hosting gymnasts in her tummy!

"Are the rest of the English Roses here, too?" he asked, glancing around.

"Yep!" Amy said cheerfully, as the vendor handed her a bag of peanuts. "I'm just buying these nuts for Charlotte's little bro—"

Ryan lightly touched Amy's arm. A lightning bolt rushed through her body. "Hey, maybe Ashton and I can hang out with you guys before the show starts?" he asked. "We can watch the performers warm up."

"Sure!" Amy beamed. Inside, her mind was racing. *Ryan-Hudson-is-sitting-with-us, Ryan-Hudson-is-sitting-with-us, ohmygod, ohmygod.*

Ryan whistled to his friend (He whistled! Amy couldn't believe his level of smoothness!), the equally debonair Ashton Cleeves.

"Hey, Amy." Ashton smiled. "What's up?"

"Not much, Ashton." Amy grinned back. "C'mon, let's find the others."

The two boys followed Amy to the circus ring, where the other Roses were standing. Amy looked over at Charlotte, Grace, Nicole, and Binah, who looked fairly startled to see her with two of the cutest boys in school. (They weren't completely shocked, though—Amy was a popular girl.)

"Hey, girls, look who I just ran into in the—"

"NUTS! WHERE ARE MY NUTS?" Amy was rudely interrupted by Patrick's overwhelming screeching.

"They're right here, Patrick," Amy said huffily, handing him the bag of roasted treats. She couldn't resist adding, "What do you say?"

Patrick look mystified. "What?"

"What do you say when someone buys something for you?"

Patrick scrunched his face into a sickeningly sweet smile, sticking his grubby hand in the bag and

fishing out a handful of nuts. "Thank yo-u-u-u," he crooned in a singsong voice. As soon as Amy turned her back, he stuck out his tongue.

"Patrick, honestly . . ." Charlotte sounded exasperated but quickly regained her composure. She smoothed her hair, straightened her skirt, and turned to the boys. "Just ignore him."

Patrick didn't seem to ruffle Ryan's relaxed demeanor in the least! "It's cool," Ryan said.

Ryan and Ashton parked themselves next to Nicole and Grace.

"There's room for you right here, Red," Ryan said, giving Amy a wink.

The man in Amy's stomach began doing backflips again. That Ryan Hudson! What he could do to a poor girl's tummy!

Suddenly, she felt a sharp jab on her lower back. Amy whirled around to that rascal Patrick laughing and making kissy faces at her. The nerve!

She turned back around, determined not to let the little monster ruin her lovely time at the circus with such fabulous friends and the cutest boy in school.

"So," she began, turning to Ryan. "Can you believe those lion tamers? How do they have the nerve to be around such beasts every day? I mean, after that one incident that happened in America with those two, you know, Siegfried and what's-his-name, you'd think—"

"Ewwwwwww!"

Patrick was moaning and groaning behind her.

"What is it this time, Patrick?" Charlotte hissed.

"Someone made a stinky smell." Patrick giggled, holding his nose. "From their . . . bum!"

Amy spun around in a fury. This time she'd had it. Embarrassing Charlotte by screaming was one thing, but interrupting her own private time with Ryan Hudson was quite another. "Patrick!" she fumed, shaking her fist. "Will you please cut it—"

"AMY MADE THE SMELL!" Patrick howled, still holding his nose with one hand while frantically pointing at Amy with the other. "AMY MADE A STINKY SMELL!"

Amy's face slowly turned the same shade of red as her hair. Panicked, she turned to her friends,

whose faces only mirrored her own look of horror. She glanced over at Ryan and Ashton. They were trying to appear straight-faced, but she could tell they were hiding snickers behind their hands.

Amy wanted to die. She wanted to crawl under the bleachers and die! Well, wouldn't you, too? *Quel* beast!

It was the kind of moment that seems tailor-made for a personal rewind button. I mean, don't you ever wish you had your own personal rewind button? You could simply press it after any humiliating, gag-yourself moment and—presto!—you're back where you started, just as if said humiliating, gag-yourself moment never even happened. Such a button would be simply marvy. The scientific community really needs to start paying attention to the

needs of twelve-year-old girls. Now, what was I saying? Oh yes . . .

At long last, Grace's voice cut through the embarrassed silence. "Hey, Patrick," she said, grabbing his arm. "Have you ever heard of the saying, 'You smelled it, you dealt it?' Seems like you're the one to blame, buddy."

Patrick look baffled. He thought for a moment. "No, I never heard that."

"Well, that's what everyone says in Atlanta, where I'm from. Say, did you see the arcade when we first walked in? I bet I can beat you in Dragon Ball!"

Patrick shook his head furiously. "No way! Cannot!"

"Can, too!" Grace taunted. "Come on, race you

there!" She hopped up, grabbed Patrick's hand, and they were off. Amy shot her a look of gratitude and mouthed, "Thank you." Grace winked. See? It really does pay to have the best friends ever.

When they were gone, Charlotte heaved a huge sigh. "I'm so, so sorry, everybody," she said sadly. "What can I say? He's not human. In fact, I'm not sure what he is."

Ashton turned around. "He's pretty bad, but I have one at home who's worse."

"Oh, really?" Binah asked, interested. "How old?"

"Well, Nino is ten," Ashton replied. "But he's already a delinquent. I swear, he'll be behind bars by the time he's our age."

"Oh yeah, Nino's a trip," Ryan joined in. "Remember the time he put hair removal stuff in your mum's shampoo bottle?"

"Ohhhh geez." Amy gasped, nervously touching her own curly red locks. "I can't believe that! Did her hair, like, fall out?"

"A little bit," Ashton admitted. "But she found out before too much damage was done—and Nino was out of commission for the entire summer."

Amy looked appalled. (You must remember that she had the school's most coveted red curls, after all, so she found such stories especially troubling.) What if her new sibling tried to pull such a stunt?

"What's with the face, Red?" Ryan teased. "You look like you've just seen a freak show!"

Amy managed a smile. "Oh, it's nothing, really. It's just that my mum is having a baby soon, so I'm kind of worried about, you know, tales of terror."

Ashton waved his hand in the air nonchalantly. "Oh, it's no biggie, really," he insisted. "Most little brothers and sisters are dweebaholics. You get used to it."

The lights dimmed, and drumrolls thundered overhead, signaling the start of the show. Amy felt the same surge of excitement that everyone (yes, even sixth graders) gets when a circus is about to begin. But then Patrick's shrill voice rang out as everybody found his or her seat, and no one—not even Siegfried and what's-his-name—could have tamed the dreadful feeling inside of her.

CHAPTER 7

It's Time!

an "accident!"

The rest of the circus went by without too much unwanted fanfare—except, of course, when Patrick's chewing gum "accidentally" (or so he said) found its way into Nicole's ponytail.

Charlotte was absolutely livid during the car ride home (luckily, Patrick insisted on riding up front next to Royston). None of the other Roses had ever seen her so vexed. Her usually pale cheeks were an angry red; her nostrils flared like those of her pet pony, Posie; and Amy even noticed a tiny vein popping out on her forehead.

"Mum. Owes. Me. Big. Time," she muttered through clenched teeth.

"Oh, Charlie, he's not that bad," Binah whispered helpfully. "Not compared to most six-year-olds."

"Not that bad?" Charlotte shrieked. "He was terrible!"

Binah glanced over at Amy, who was stone-faced. "What's wrong, Aim?" she asked in a concerned tone.

Amy shook her head. How could she possibly

explain all the terrible thoughts going through her head? Her mum was having a baby—wasn't that a good thing? Wasn't she supposed to be happy and excited and proud and all of those other nice things a big sister should be? Somehow, she couldn't make herself feel anything but lousy.

"I don't know, guys. I guess I'm just scared. I mean, my mum is due any day now, and that means everything is going to change. My life, as I know it, will be over. What if I'm expected to babysit all the time? I don't think I could handle . . . that!" She gestured toward Patrick, who was busy making unpleasant sounds with his armpit.

Grace put her arm around Amy. "You can't worry about that now. Who knows what your little bro or sis will be like?"

"That's true," Charlotte chimed in. "I mean, I do have to deal with Patrick, but then, look at Emma and I! We get along splendidly!"

"And you already have Chloe," Binah added. "She's not bad at all."

"But Chloe was born so long ago," Amy explained. "I can hardly remember when she was a baby, because I was only two when she was born! But this one," she sighed dramatically," this one will probably turn out to be a total spoiled brat."

"I don't think that's going to happen," Grace reassured her. "Not with a fabulous older sister like you."

"That's a good point," Nicole added. "Plus, I read somewhere that the wider the age difference, the better that siblings get along with each other."

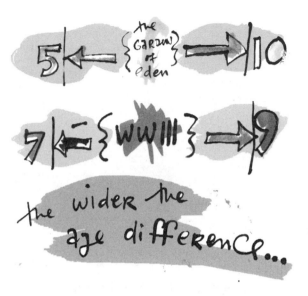

"Really?" asked Amy hopefully. She paused. "But what if my mum doesn't have any time for me after the baby is born? I mean, we have so much fun together, and she's going to be so busy. She didn't even have time to tell me which shoes to wear today; what if she doesn't need me anymore?"

The littlest Rose

Amy suddenly realized that this was her very worst fear.

"Oh, Amy," Grace said, putting her arm around her friend and giving her a gentle squeeze. "Your mom's feelings for you aren't going to change just because she has a baby."

"Yeah," Charlotte added. "She has enough love to go round. I'm sure of it."

"Me, too," Binah chimed in. Binah, whose mum died when she was very little, was especially sensitive to such matters. "Your mum will be there for you no matter what."

"Really," Nicole reassured her. She put her hands on Amy's shoulders and looked her square in the eyes. "I know that everything is going to be okay."

By this time, Royston had pulled into the

Ginsbergs' driveway and turned off the car. Patrick hopped out of the car and was making a beeline for the front door, screaming about God-knows-what. "Do you girls wanna come inside for a bit?" Charlotte asked. "I'll make sure that Patrick gets lost," she added.

The girls were just about to respond when Amy's cell phone started going crazy.

"Sorry!" she said, digging through her massive bag. What can I say? Amy's not the most organized one of the group.

"Hello," she answered. "Hi, Richard. WHAT? NOW? OH MY, OH MY . . ."

The other girls looked at one another with shocked expressions.

"Yes, I'll be right there," Amy said solemnly. She clicked off her phone and stared at the Roses. "My mum . . . my mum's in labor. She's at the hospital. I have to go. Like, NOW!"

Charlotte sprang into action. "I'll have Royston drive you," she said, running into the house.

The rest of the Roses gathered around their friend, sweeping her into a giant hug.

"Good luck!" Binah grinned.

"It's going to be okay, Amy, really," Grace said. "You're an awesome big sister."

"Call us as soon as you hear anything!" Charlotte gushed, pushing Amy into the car.

Amy gulped. She didn't know what she was in for, but there was no time to think about it. The baby was officially on its way—whether she liked it or not!

CHAPTER 8

Blinking-Baby Blues

"Amy," Chloe whined, tugging at the sleeve of her sister's sweatshirt. "I'm bo-o-red. What's going on in there?" She motioned toward the big white doors at the end of the waiting room.

"Chloe," Amy said, exasperated. "For the millionth time, Mum is in labor. Richard will come out and tell us as soon as there's any news!" She tried to return to her *Vogue*, but it was proving impossible. Irritated as she was with Chloe's constant nagging, she had to admit that the suspense was killing her, too. It had been three hours already, and no news!

She kept thinking about the events of the day. The English Roses were so sure that everything was going to be okay—that her mum would have time for the new baby and her, too. But what if they were wrong?

Amy didn't have time to contemplate further. Just then, Richard burst through the doors, wearing a smile that seemed to make his face light up from the inside (and for once, Amy couldn't help but note, he wasn't wearing his boring pinstriped suit).

"IT'S A GIRL!" he shrieked, running over to both Amy and Chloe and wrapping them in a warm embrace. "Congratulations! You have a beautiful little sister."

Amy felt shaky, and to her surprise, even a bit teary. She couldn't remember ever seeing dull Richard this filled with life before.

"When can I see Mum?" Amy asked, pulling away.

"Your mum's resting now," he said. "But why don't we all take a walk and visit your new sister? As soon as I get something in my stomach," he added eagerly. "I'm starving."

They made a quick trip to the hospital cafeteria and, ten minutes later, Amy held Chloe's hand as

they followed Richard to the observation room. They stopped in front of a big glass window. On the other side of the window was a room filled with tiny cradles. And in each cradle laid a wriggling newborn baby.

"But . . . but how do we know which one is ours?" Chloe asked tearfully.

"She's that one." Richard pointed to the third row, second from the left. "The one with all the hair," he added with a silly grin.

Amy pressed her face to the glass. The baby Richard pointed to—her new sister—had skin that looked as soft and delicate as tissue paper. Her tiny hands—complete with ten itsy-bitsy fingernails— wriggled and grasped at the air. But best of all, she had a thick crop of reddish hair. Crazy hair. Wild hair, just like Amy's. She opened her eyes, which were a beautiful, deep blue, just like Amy's mum's, and yawned. And then she looked right at Amy.

"She looked at me," Amy marveled excitedly. "I mean, she looked directly at me!"

"No way!" Chloe said, poking Amy in the ribs. "That's impossible. You're making it up."

Amy sighed and, once again, pressed her face against the glass. Nestled among blankets, little sister stretched and blinked her sweet blue eyes. And at that very moment, something in Amy seemed to click inside.

"She's . . . lovely," Amy breathed. "Absolutely lovely. Like an angel."

CHAPTER 9

The Next Fashion Star!

Amy gently knocked on the hospital room door.

"Come in," came her mother's muffled voice. Amy slowly opened the door to find her mother lying in bed. The room was filled with sunlight and the fresh scent of flowers from well-wishers. At the sound of the door latch, her mum stirred and sat up. "Amy-Paimey," she said brightly, "is that you?" She held out her arms, and Amy ran into them.

"I'm so, so happy to see my number one girl," she said. "I missed you!"

"I missed you, too, Mum," Amy said. Suddenly, something seemed to break inside. She didn't know why, but she felt tears coming to her eyes.

"What's wrong, sweetie?" her mum soothed, brushing Amy's tears away. "I know, I know," she said, answering her own question. "It's been a lo-ong day."

Amy laughed. "It's been even longer for you!" she said, wiping her face. "How are you feeling?"

"Better now that you're here," she said. "But this

hospital gown—ick!" She made a face. "There must be something more attractive they could have us wear in here."

Amy laughed. Suddenly, she wanted more than anything to tell her mum just what she had been feeling. And the words poured out of her.

"Mum, I'm so sorry," she said. "I was jealous. . . . I was scared that the baby would take up all of your time. And then today, we had to take Charlie's little brother to the circus, and he was a nightmare, and . . . and all I could think was that this little monster was going to come into my life and ruin it and you would never, ever have time for me anymore!"

Amy's mum cupped her daughter's chin in her hand. "Honey, I will never, ever not have time for you. I couldn't survive without you!"

"Really?" Amy asked.

"Really," her mum said. "In fact, I'm going to need your help more than ever with this baby. But that doesn't mean that I won't have time to do any of our usual things—our shopping trips and lunches and even traveling. I'm the same mum that you've always had! And I love you very much."

Amy hugged her mother so tightly, she thought she would burst. Her mum had said the words she needed to hear—that she couldn't survive without her.

"Did you see the baby yet?" Amy's mum asked.

"Yes," Amy replied.

"And what did you think?"

"I-I simply adore her, Mum," Amy admitted. "I can't imagine loving anything more. She's just perfect."

Amy's mum smiled. "She is, Aim. Almost as perfect as you! She has your hair!" She laughed. "We've been considering the name Stella. What do you think?"

"Stella," Amy repeated. "Oh, Mum, I love it! She could be the next Stella McCartney."

"No, *you're* going to be the next Stella McCartney," her mother corrected. "But you could teach her everything you know. And you should be learning a lot at Spring Fashion Week in Milan, because I'm taking you!"

Amy gasped. "What? No way, Mum, are you serious?"

"Yes!" Her mum laughed. "I wanted it to be a surprise for your birthday in August, but I just couldn't wait to tell you. Do you think it could make up for missing Fall Fashion Week?"

Amy thought that it just might!

CHAPTER 10

The Best Big Sis

After Amy had sat with her mother for a little longer and filled her in on her recent adventure at the circus with Patrick (Amy's mother couldn't help but laugh out loud, and Amy had to admit the story sounded very funny now that it was over), there was another soft knock at the door. In walked Chloe, with Richard right behind her.

"Hey, Mummy," Chloe said, plopping down on the bed and wrapping her arms around their mother.

Richard sat down in the chair next to Amy's; and for some reason, Amy suddenly felt very shy. He gently placed his hand on Amy's back. He cleared his throat nervously. "I'm glad that we're all here together," he offered timidly.

Amy looked at her mother, whose eyes were shining with happiness. "Me, too," Amy declared. And as she saw Richard and her mum stare at each other with so much love in their eyes, Amy knew that she was. After all, if he made her mum so happy, maybe Richard wasn't such a bore.

Just then, the nurse wheeled in a small carriage. "Feeding time," she declared, lifting the small, wriggling bundle that was Amy's brand-new sister and placing her carefully into Amy's mother's arms.

"Wait a minute," Amy's mum interrupted. "Amy, do you want to hold her?"

Amy nodded, and her mum transferred the baby into her arms. Amy took a deep breath. She had to admit that it was a bit frightening to hold this tiny, helpless thing. She was almost afraid that if she moved the wrong way, Stella would break.

Richard and Chloe began describing to Amy's mother the horrors of the hospital cafeteria. "The pudding looked like melted crayons!" Chloe proclaimed excitedly.

As her family laughed and talked, Amy rocked the baby in her arms. *Hey, this isn't so hard,* she thought. Moving away from the group, she whispered, "Hi, Stella. I'm your big sister. And I'm sorry if I wasn't exactly thrilled about you coming at first. But now I know I'm going to be the best oldest sister in the whole, wide world. And I'm going to show you the ways of the stylin'. Because you're way better than Milan Fashion Week!"

She looked down at her little sister, who suddenly opened her eyes and, Amy was positive, gave her a teeny, tiny smile.

The End

Once upon a time, the five most fabulous girls in London were the five most adorable babies in London!

ℰBinah

is rocking her favorite doll to sleep—the same doll
she loves today!

Nicole

is reaching for the stars at only six months old!

Charlotte

is posing for the camera like a true starlet.

Grace

is chasing after her brothers' football.

Amy

is already an accessories expert!

MADONNA RITCHIE was born in Bay City, Michigan, and now lives in London and Los Angeles with her husband, movie director Guy Ritchie, and her children, Lola, Rocco, and David. She has recorded 17 albums and appeared in 18 movies. This is the fifth in her series of chapter books. She has also written six picture books for children, starting with the international bestseller *The English Roses*, which was released in 40 languages and more than 100 countries.

JEFFREY FULVIMARI was born in Akron, Ohio. He started coloring when he was two, and has never stopped. Soon after graduating from The Cooper Union in New York City, he began drawing for magazines and television commercials around the globe. He currently lives in a log cabin in upstate New York, and is happiest when surrounded by stacks of paper and magic markers.